Roger Williams writes for theatre, radio and television. Credits include the BAFTA-nominated *Tales From Pleasure Beach* for BBC2, *The Story of Tracy Beaker* for BBC1 and *Pobol Y Cwm* for S4C. He has written theatre plays for Made In Wales (*Gulp*), The Sherman (*Saturday Night Forever*) and The Royal Welsh College of Music and Drama (*Y Byd (A'i Brawd)*), and five radio plays for the BBC. He is thirty years old and lives in Carmarthenshire.

Mother Tongue

Roger Williams

PARTHIAN

first night drama

Parthian
The Old Surgery
Napier Street
Cardigan
SA43 1ED

www.parthianbooks.co.uk

First published in 2005
© Roger Williams 2005
All Rights Reserved

ISBN 1-902638-79-4
      9781902638799

Cover design by Anne Cakebread & Lucy Llewellyn
Typeset by type@lloydrobson.com
Printed and bound by Dinefwr Press, Llandybïe, Wales

Published with the financial support of the Welsh
Books Council

British Library Cataloguing in Publication Data – A
cataloguing record for this book is available from the
British Library

Mother Tongue *was written with financial support from the Arts Council of Wales & Wales Arts International.*

Mother Tongue

First performed at Chapter Arts Centre, Cardiff
13 July 2005.

Cast:

Joel – Stephen Marzella
A thirty-eight year old American man

Nangarra – Sandra Kelly
A thirty-nine year old Aboriginal Australian woman

Gail – Sharon Morgan
*A forty-nine year old woman – twenty-five years spent living in
London have made it hard to recognise her Celtic accent*

Amos – Victor Rodger
A thirty-five year old Polynesian man

Creative Team:

Director – James Tyson
Designer – Paul Rees
Assistant Director – Alexander Ferris

James Tyson would like to thank Yirri Yaakin Theatre
Company, Australia, and Carla Van Zon at the New Zealand
International Arts Festival, for their assistance with casting
this production.

The play is set in various locations in and around present day
Cardiff.

Act One

Scene One

Lights rise to reveal a smartly dressed JOEL giving a presentation to a conference.

JOEL: Popular thinking would have us believe that television is threatening cultural diversity. I turn this argument on its head, and suggest to you that TV actually has the power to promote diversity. I would even go so far as saying that television could save our world's smaller cultures. Let me tell you how: digital technology. With the onset of multi-streaming it will soon be possible for viewers to choose the language in which they wish to watch programmes. Yarru, Mandaya, Tierro... take your pick! For the first time in history, English no longer needs to be the dominant language of American broadcasting. And we, ladies and gentlemen, could be at the forefront of the revolution.

Blackout.

Scene Two

A telephone rings. Lights rise to reveal NANGARRA making a call on a public telephone in an airport arrivals hall. The ringing comes to an abrupt end as the call is answered.

NANGARRA: Jen? It's Nan. Yeah. Got here in one piece. How's Marra? (*Beat.*) Make sure she takes her medication hey? And get the doctor if anything... call if anything comes up, anything at all, okay? (*Beat.*) Is Marra there? Put her on,

will you? Ta. (*Pause. Softly, she speaks her own language.*) Marra?
Nangarra. Ganga sirri gara. Iwi jarra ganga. Ganga sirri.
Marra? (*Beat.*) Iwi jarra ganga.

Blackout.

Scene Three

*A luxury hotel suite on the top floor of a five-star Cardiff hotel.
Comfortable sofas, a coffee table, a half-bottle of champagne on ice,
glasses, a telephone, and a bank of large glass windows looking out
across the city. JOEL stands looking out through the windows with his
whole body pressed up against the glass. GAIL enters from the hall,
stops, and watches him. GAIL's holding a glass tumbler. She drinks.*

GAIL: I hope you're not thinking of jumping. You'll leave a
terrible mess on the pavement. They'll be scraping bits of
you up for weeks to come. (*She smiles, and rattles the ice in her
glass.*)

JOEL: They're sealed shut. They've obviously considered
every eventuality.

GAIL: The sign of a good five-star hotel. 'Fully stocked
mini-bar, satellite TV and sealed windows to make sure the
guests don't do anything foolish after that fifth bottle of
champagne, (*Beat.*) So, it's true. The big guns really are in
town.

JOEL: If by 'big guns' you mean me Gail, then yes, I'm in
town. But I'd argue with you over my billing.

4

GAIL: This must be a very important conference to attract the personal attendance of Mr Joel Stuart. Don't you usually send one of your minions?

JOEL: Ordinarily. But when I saw your name on the list....

GAIL (*laughs heartily*): Liar.

JOEL: There was the lure of a new destination also. I've never been to Wales. I hear they do great mountains, and serve a very nice drop of... water. (*Beat.*) When was the last time we...

GAIL: Collided? Madrid. Two thousand and three. Flamenco and food poisoning.

JOEL: I knew there was a reason I'd given up shellfish.

JOEL kisses GAIL on the cheek.

JOEL (*spots the glass*): Vodka?

GAIL: Gin. Even I don't hit the hard stuff before dinner.

JOEL: But gin is...

GAIL: An appetiser. (*Beat.*) How's life in la-la land?

JOEL: Been listening to the rumours have we?

GAIL: Beach house overlooking the Pacific and a hot-tub by all accounts. True, or false?

JOEL: Well firstly, the place I've bought is not a house but an apartment, and secondly, the new pad is at least two miles from the beach. So, 'beach house'? I don't think so. You know how much we linguists earn.

GAIL: You've always done very well for yourself.

JOEL: I'm careful.

GAIL: You're canny. I've watched your unprecedented rise from PhD student to leading light in the world of linguistics. That sort of success doesn't happen without some... creativity.

JOEL: That's a nice way of putting it.

GAIL: So, tell me, Joel. What big idea brings you to Cardiff?

JOEL: What're my chances of getting a decent cup of coffee in this place?

GAIL: Avoidance techniques.

JOEL: Does the word 'espresso' mean anything in Wales?

GAIL waits for an answer.

JOEL: You don't expect me to give away my secrets, do you?

GAIL: I'll find out eventually.

JOEL: Eventually, yes. But this is a competition for one-point-four million dollars, and I'm not about to sleep with the enemy, am I?

They look at one another ambiguously.

JOEL: Do you know the other finalists?

GAIL: I know Amos. Met him last month in Auckland.

JOEL: What's he like?

GAIL: Are you really asking me to believe you haven't looked him up on the net?

JOEL: I'm interested in your opinion.

GAIL: Well, he's handsome, talented, younger than you.... (*GAIL smiles at JOEL.*) Amos is an impressive figure. Passionate, respected in Polynesia.... (*Beat.*) So, if you've moved to California you're probably working with Native Americans? Correct?

JOEL: Nice try.

GAIL: Come on Joel. We're old pals. Spill the beans.

JOEL: Patience, Gail. You'll just have to wait until...

GAIL: You win the money?

JOEL smiles.

GAIL: Cocky little...

JOEL: Like you say, I've come far in a relatively short space of time. Confidence helps.

GAIL: Bullshit.

JOEL: Call it what you like. It's a successful formula.

Beat.

GAIL: Don't know the fourth applicant. The Aborigine. But to be frank I don't know why they're bothering to pay the poor cow's airfare.

JOEL: Not a very optimistic view from a linguist such as yourself, Mrs Richmond.

GAIL: Come off it! This conference isn't going to award one-point-four million dollars to a language that'll probably be dead in three years time when the last four speakers die in a car crash or something equally as trivial.

JOEL: Don't hold back, Gail.

GAIL: One head on collision – language wiped out. It's very sad. Some of those languages are the most complex ever spoken by man, and they're dying. By the middle of this century there'll be what? Fifteen left! Out of two hundred and fifty! Honestly! Waste of bloody time. (*She drains her glass.*) Can I get you a sniffter?

JOEL: No thanks.

GAIL: Small whisky? Cheeky G'n'T?

GAIL comes up close to JOEL.

GAIL: Not even a quick one?

Pause. They kiss. GAIL pulls back momentarily. She smiles.

GAIL: Nice to see you again, Joel.

They stare at one another. Beat. AMOS enters holding his key-card.

AMOS: Gail! D'you know what? For one terrible minute there I thought I'd lost my key. Again. It's their own fault really, if they didn't make them look like business cards, I wouldn't keep giving them away to people. I've got one for my room, the gym, this place, the com.... (*munication centre*)

GAIL: Hello, Amos. Didn't think I'd be seeing you so soon.

They shake hands.

AMOS: Yes, it was quite a shock for me too. Something I said in the proposal must've pushed the right buttons I guess. There's an art to filling those forms in, isn't there? Or at least, a skill. Of sorts. A method maybe.

AMOS and JOEL look at one another for the first time.

GAIL: Amos, this is Joel Stuart. Joel, Amos Fraser.

AMOS: Joel Stuart. Burton College. I've read your papers. Very impressive. The last article on generational language shifts was excellent.

JOEL and AMOS shake hands.

JOEL: Thank you.

AMOS: Honestly, really good.

JOEL: Yeah. I know.

Pause. AMOS doesn't know how to react to JOEL's confidence. Then, at last, he laughs loudly, and belatedly.

JOEL: When did you get in, Amos?

AMOS: Two days ago. Or was it three? Just when I think I'm kicking the jet-lag...

GAIL: It comes back to kick you.

AMOS: I wanted to get here early to do some detective work. You read so much about how successfully the Welsh have managed to hold onto their language I thought I'd see the initiatives first hand.

GAIL: Very industrious of you.

AMOS: All part of this new job I've got. Did I tell you about it when we were in Auckland, Gail? Did I even have it then? Maybe not. Sorry. Lost my thread. I'm the government's officer for Thiai now. In charge of language promotion.

JOEL: Congratulations.

AMOS: Sounds much more important than it is. I head a

department of one. Can you have a department of one? I don't know. Probably not. But it's me, a computer, and a secretary who comes in two days a week.

JOEL: Going all out, aren't they?

AMOS: I share her. With the Office of Parks and Recreation. Monday and Wednesday with me. Tuesday and Thursday with them.

GAIL: What does she do on Friday?

AMOS: It's her day off. (*Beat.*) I know it doesn't seem like much, but after years of neglect Thiai is finally gaining some official status. That's where the Welsh have got it right. Reckon we could all learn a few lessons from their success.

JOEL: Indeed. Whoever said the Welsh weren't an assertive race hadn't met a language campaigner.

AMOS: Bilingual road signs, broadcasting, huge sums of government subsidy... it's all very impressive.

GAIL: And yet you've got to wonder how much of it is absolutely necessary.

AMOS: Sorry?

GAIL: Well, do they *really* need to spend thousands of pounds on signage telling us where the toilets are in two languages?

AMOS: I suppose they'd argue it was about equality.

GAIL: Of course they would. But if the Welsh were truly clever they'd save their money, and put their signs up solely in Welsh. I'm sure the monoglots in the hotel would find the fire exit when push came to shove.

Pause. AMOS once again isn't sure how to react. He once again takes the comments as a joke and laughs loudly.

AMOS: Push. Shove. I see what you.... (*Beat.*) Has anyone seen Nangarra?

GAIL: You know her?

AMOS: Sure. We studied together in Canberra.

JOEL: Gail was just saying, before you arrived that is Amos, how concerned she is about the fate of the Australian languages. She's looking forward to discussing the subject with Nangarra. In depth. (*Beat.*) Aren't you Gail?

GAIL: Can't wait.

AMOS: Nan will be more than happy to give you the low down, Gail. She can talk the leg off a donkey when it comes to Gurru Gurru.

GAIL: Drink anyone?

AMOS: Oh, I don't know. It's a bit early for me to be honest.

GAIL lifts up the half-bottle of champagne from the ice bucket.

GAIL: Oh, come on Amos. You're not going to let me drink

this entire bottle all by myself, are you?

AMOS: Oh, go on then. One glass. What harm can it do?

GAIL hands AMOS the bottle to open. GAIL goes for the glasses.

GAIL: That's the spirit. Joel? Can I tempt you?

JOEL: Thanks Gail, but I'm...

GAIL: Nonsense! A conference wouldn't be a conference if we didn't drink the mini-bar dry.

AMOS pops the bottle open. GAIL gives a shout as the cork comes out. They start to fill the glasses. The door swings open. NANGARRA enters fresh from a twenty-four hour flight. JOEL and NANGARRA's eyes meet. AMOS spots NANGARRA.

AMOS: Nan!

AMOS and NANGARRA embrace. GAIL pours the champagne.

AMOS: I was starting to think you weren't going to make it.

NANGARRA: Funny. Almost didn't. There's still a question mark over my bags.

AMOS: Bad trip?

NANGARRA: Delays, lost luggage, the only seat on the plane that wouldn't recline... it couldn't have been much worse.

GAIL is handing out the glasses of champagne.

GAIL: Oh, I don't know... you could've crashed.

NANGARRA glares at GAIL in astonishment.

GAIL: Gail Richmond. How d'you do?

NANGARRA: Nangarra Yinpungu.

GAIL: We were just chatting about you actually.

NANGARRA: Thought my ears were burning.

GAIL: Amos was filling us in on your past.

AMOS: All good. Cross my heart.

JOEL (*steps forward to introduce himself*): Joel Stuart.

NANGARRA and JOEL shake hands.

JOEL: Australian, right?

Beat.

NANGARRA: No. What makes you think that, mate?

JOEL, for once, doesn't know how to respond. Beat. AMOS breaks the silence with a raucous burst of laughter.

Blackout.

Scene Four

The roof-garden of a smart wine bar in central Cardiff. The sound of a party in progress. NANGARRA and AMOS appear laughing with cocktails. AMOS looks over the balcony and NANGARRA lights a cigarette.

AMOS: We're safe. She didn't see us come out here.

NANGARRA: Are you sure she was coming on to you?

AMOS: Too right! She had that look, y'know?

NANGARRA: No.

AMOS: Staring me deep in the eyes....

NANGARRA: Ah, *that* look.

AMOS: Her pupils dilated. That look of expec... tation.

NANGARRA: Any other tell tale signs?

AMOS: She licked her lips.

NANGARRA: Maybe she was hungry.

AMOS: That's what worries me.

They laugh.

NANGARRA: Amos, mate. Wouldn't it be easier if you just told her you're a woofter?

AMOS: I couldn't get a word in edgeways. She asked me if I fancied a bit of slap and tickle but I couldn't hear her above the music, so I thought she was asking if I wanted to try the crab and pickle.

NANGARRA: You didn't say 'yes'?

AMOS: A misunderstanding!

NANGARRA: Well, no wonder the girl thinks she's on a promise!

AMOS: It's not funny! Let's stay here until she finds someone else to play with, eh?

NANGARRA: Tell her to piss off.

AMOS: I can't. She's on the judging panel for the grant.

NANGARRA: Well, in that case, maybe you *should* screw her. I'm sure Nathan wouldn't mind.

AMOS: Nathan and I split up.

NANGARRA: No way!

AMOS: It was all very adult. He kept the flat, I got the microwave.

NANGARRA: What happened?

AMOS: He took out a gym membership. Late last year Nathan decided to bulk up. But rather than letting nature take its course, he started taking protein powders. He didn't want to firm up you see, but beef up, and with these protein powders his chest just popped up. Boom! Instant pecs.

NANGARRA: Must've been fun.

AMOS: You'd reckon! But Nathan started spending more and more time at the gym and less time at home. We grew apart and found we didn't have anything to say to each other. Days went by without conversation. The odd word, yes, a sentence maybe, but we never talked. The bigger he got, the less he had to tell me. We tried to keep things going, but... well... his tits got in the way.

NANGARRA: So you're cooking for one again are you?

AMOS: Not exactly. There's Hone.

NANGARRA: Don't waste much time, d'you?

AMOS: He's lovely. Maori, big biceps, lots of tattoos. When people meet him in the street they get a bit intimidated, y'know? It's like he's this big giant of a guy everyone's afraid of. But at home it's a completely different story.

NANGARRA: Carpet slippers and Judy Garland?

AMOS: Elton John. (*Beat.*) What about you? Got anyone on bush patrol at the moment?

NANGARRA: Amos!

AMOS: Well?

NANGARRA: No! (*Beat.*) You know my problem, don't you? Tony was everything I wanted. Gurru Gurru, clever, good looking... big dick.

AMOS: Amen!

NANGARRA: Nobody measures up. Truth be told, I'd be happier with a baby than a bloke. Come to think of it, there's not a lot of difference is there?

AMOS: You never know. You might meet someone at the conference.

NANGARRA: Stop right there!

AMOS: What?

NANGARRA: You might be looking for a conference shag Amos, but I'm not.

AMOS: Moi? Conference shag?

NANGARRA: Don't deny it! I've seen you flirting with him.

AMOS: Who?

NANGARRA: I can tell when you're on a mission. You drop your shoulders and you suck your stomach in. Joel Stuart, indeed. And I thought you had taste.

AMOS: He's gorgeous! Haven't you seen his arse?

NANGARRA: Course I have. He talks out of it.

AMOS: Give him a chance. Get to know him.

NANGARRA: I don't want to get to know him. Do you know how many languages he's worked with in the course of his career?

AMOS: No, but...

NANGARRA: Neither does he! You must've heard what he did with the Maearra language?

AMOS: I know there were stories, but...

NANGARRA: A global multi-national, which has threatened to sue if the rumour is repeated publicly again...

AMOS: Gossip...

NANGARRA: Paid Joel Stuart to go into South America and persuade a number of languages to include the letter 'K' in their official alphabets. He did this for a fee I've heard, of eighty thousand dollars. Joel decided it was essential for these languages to have the letter 'K' in their alphabets not because they necessarily needed it, but because without the letter 'K' how else could they manage the essential terms we all need in the new century such as Starbucks? Nike? Reebok? Coke?

AMOS: Fuck.

NANGARRA: Exactly! And you want to suck this man's dick?

AMOS: Well, yes, but I want him to suck mine too.

JOEL enters.

JOEL: Not interrupting, am I?

AMOS: No, not at all. We were just talking about, erm... language, linguistics... weren't we Nan?

NANGARRA: No, Amos. We were talking about men.

AMOS laughs.

JOEL: It's just that there's a policeman here to see you, Amos.

NANGARRA: Policeman?

JOEL: The concierge at the hotel said you were here. He's out front.

AMOS: Then I'd better go and see what he wants.

NANGARRA: Need me to come with you mate?

AMOS: Nah. I'll be right. Just promise to come looking for me if I'm not back for breakfast, eh?

AMOS leaves.

JOEL: What were you two *really* talking about?

NANGARRA: Secret women's business. If I told you I'd have to kill you.

JOEL: Better not then, hey? (*Beat.*) Queensland, right? Brisbane?

NANGARRA: You know Australia?

JOEL: Kind of. I've been to Sydney.

NANGARRA: For the Indigenous Language Conference?

JOEL: No. The Olympics. (*Beat.*) Amos says you're a native speaker of Gurru Gurru.

NANGARRA: Mother tongue.

JOEL: You're a rare species then.

NANGARRA: But a hardy one.

JOEL: And your language is going to survive?

NANGARRA: If I've got anything to do with it. English is an imported language to Australia from a cold grey island thousands of miles away. How can it ever describe my country? That's why winning the grant this weekend is so important.

JOEL: Yeah, well. There are four of us thinking exactly the same thing. (*Beat.*) Feeling nervous?

NANGARRA: Are you?

JOEL: Not particularly.

NANGARRA: Then, neither am I.

GAIL enters, tipsy.

GAIL: Joel, you naughty litt.... (*Beat.*) Oh, Nangarra. Enjoying the party?

NANGARRA: Having a ball, thanks. Are you heading back?

GAIL: Yes, they've started the dancing now. Had I known, I'd never have worn these shoes. Besides, we've got a long day ahead of us tomorrow. Should get a good night's rest really. Joel and I are going to share a taxi back to the hotel. (*Beat.*) Would you care to join us?

Pause.

NANGARRA: No thanks. I'll wait for Amos.

GAIL: Very well... goodnight, then.

NANGARRA: Night.

GAIL: Joel?

JOEL: See you tomorrow.

AMOS enters.

AMOS: Oh, are you leaving?

GAIL: Yes, early start you know?

JOEL: Night.

AMOS: Sleep well.

GAIL and JOEL leave.

NANGARRA: Somehow Amos, I don't reckon there'll be much sleeping going on.

AMOS: You don't...

NANGARRA: I'd say it was a sure thing.

AMOS: Bitch!

NANGARRA: Bit of competition never harmed anyone.

AMOS: I knew I shouldn't have let him out of my sight.

NANGARRA: What did your policeman want?

AMOS: It's a long story.

NANGARRA: I like long stories.

AMOS: It's nothing really.

NANGARRA: Amos.

AMOS: Well, if you must know, I was arrested this morning.

NANGARRA: Arrested! What for!

AMOS: I'm not sure really. I wasn't doing anything wrong. I wasn't following them. Not in the way the cops thought anyway.

NANGARRA: Following them?

AMOS: Yeah. The girls. Besides, the cops have decided not to take the matter any further so it's all academic.

NANGARRA: Whoa! Back up Amos. What exactly did you do?

AMOS: Well, I was in town this morning, flexing the plastic, when I heard these two girls talking. Talking a language I hadn't heard before, y'know? It didn't take me long to work out it was Welsh, I mean this is Wales, after all. So, you know me Nan, always interested, I listened in. True, I shouldn't have done it, but fascination got the better of me and I followed them. Down the street. Into the train station. Up the steps. All the time listening. Trying to pick out phrases and phonics. Along the platform, through the door, and before I knew it, I was standing in the middle of the women's toilets.

NANGARRA laughs out loud.

AMOS: I can't believe you think Joel and Gail are screwing!

NANGARRA: I get the impression Joel screws everyone. Now, are we going to go back inside and get pissed, or are you still being chased by your Canadian friend?

AMOS: I think the coast is clear. She's cornered the delegate

24

from Ecuador who doesn't look much older than fifteen, and apparently doesn't speak a word of English.

NANGARRA: Then why are we standing out here freezing our tits off?

Blackout.

Scene Five

GAIL's hotel bedroom. GAIL and JOEL are locked in an embrace. GAIL pulls away.

GAIL: I'm a terrible woman. No principles, at all.

JOEL: Ditto. Which is why we keep falling into bed together. (*He looks at his wristwatch.*)

GAIL: Bored of me already?

JOEL: Force of habit. I'm always up against some kind of schedule.

GAIL: You have a sex schedule? Jesus. Where's your cock due next?

JOEL: I should get back to my room.

GAIL: Why?

JOEL: I've still got some work to do for tomorrow.

GAIL: You don't have to lie to me, Joel. If you don't want to stay just...

JOEL: I'm not lying, Gail. The office is gathering some last minute information. I should read it before the presentation. (*Beat.*) There's no need to get paranoid. Any other time, I would, I'd stay, but...

GAIL: It's not every day you're bidding for one-point-four million dollars.

JOEL buttons his shirt.

GAIL: This is unlike you. I'd've thought you'd've finished your presentation weeks ago.

JOEL: I did. This is information about the other candidates. It pays to be prepared.

GAIL: Your spies have been digging into my past, have they?

JOEL: No offence Gail, but you're a known quantity. Amos and Nangarra are the new kids on the block. And you know me, I like to know everything about everyone.

GAIL: You're taking this grant seriously, aren't you?

JOEL: I always do. Besides, it's the first time they've made this award. I want to be the inaugural winner. Set the standard.

JOEL grins at GAIL.

GAIL: And have you found out anything interesting about our colleagues?

JOEL: They've come up with some very interesting facts about our Australian friend, including a conviction for criminal damage committed on a march for Aboriginal rights.

GAIL: Probably a fit up.

JOEL: More than likely. But there's also evidence that casts doubt over the actual number of living Gurru Gurru speakers. Nangarra claims there are more than two hundred and fifty speakers, but staff in the office have come across a report that brings that figure into serious doubt.

GAIL: Everyone knows how difficult it is to get reliable statistics for desert languages.

JOEL: Gail, this report claims there are at least fewer than twenty speakers of Gurru Gurru. You don't see such large differentials as that. This researcher, Connie Matthews, started to claim Nangarra's work was widely inaccurate. But when Connie started to get some attention, Nangarra came out fighting and made her life so difficult, that Matthews was forced to abandon her project. The findings were eventually published, but because they're considered incomplete, have never been taken seriously.

GAIL: So, what're you saying? Nangarra's massaged the figures?

JOEL: Who knows? Perhaps this Matthews woman was onto something and the only remaining speakers of Gurru

Gurru are actually Nangarra, her mother, and the next door neighbour's dog.

GAIL: So you haven't dug anything up about Amos, yet?

JOEL: It's amazing how anyone's life could be so dull. A text book story of a hard working, well-meaning linguist delivering results. Makes you sick. (*Beat.*) See you tomorrow?

GAIL: Sure.

JOEL: I'm sorry I have to leave, but...

GAIL: When the devil drives... I know.

JOEL: Will you be okay?

GAIL: Yes! Go. Go! Maybe I'll do some more preparation myself. For all the good it'll do me.

JOEL kisses GAIL. JOEL exits. GAIL sits in thought.

Blackout.

Scene Six

AMOS stands before the selection panel giving his presentation using cue cards.

AMOS: We know that one of the main problems facing lesser used languages is that young people – the next generation of speakers – often do not want to speak the language. This feeling stems from a number of factors. One, teenagers see it as a natural rebellion to reject their parents' language when there is an alternative at work. Two, the television programmes, cinema, and popular music they listen to are all predominantly English which makes the rebellion easier. Three, they consider their language to be of the past and to have no relevance to their modern lives. In the words of one young Thiai speaker, 'I don't wanna talk language. Language is uncool.' It is with this in mind that I want to launch 'The Sweet Project'. An initiative which will change young attitudes to Thiai, make young speakers proud to speak the language and encourage non-Thiai speakers to start learning it. After all, without the next generation of Thiai speakers... we will have no language.

Blackout.

Scene Seven

The hotel suite. NANGARRA is talking on the telephone looking out across the city.

NANGARRA: Has she eaten? Well, that's a good sign, eh? And she's taking her medication? When was the nurse last there? Then call her. Tell her to come over. Sorry, I know you're doing your best cuz. I know. And I'll be back in a couple of days. Soon as I'm done. (*Beat.*) Give my Mum a message, will you? You listening? Iwi jarra... Nah, 'course you can remember it. It's not hard. Iwi jarra... okay, get a pen and write it down the way you think you spell it. Ready? 'Iwi jarra ganga.' What? It means, 'I love you.'

NANGARRA hangs up. An uptight GAIL enters the room. She paces and fidgets nervously.

GAIL: Is Amos still in there? (*Beat.*) God, they're taking their time, aren't they? Must be giving him a good grilling. I hate these things. Interviews. Don't know why I do it anymore. Much rather be a picker than a pickee.

NANGARRA: Gail....

GAIL: You seem very calm, or are you just very good at hiding it?

NANGARRA: Why don't you sit down?

GAIL: Might as well. Don't know how long they're going to be, do we? (*She sits.*) Are you ready for the interrogation?

NANGARRA: As I'll ever be. You've done this before?

GAIL: Christ yes! More times than I care to remember. Not to this mob though obviously. I don't know what they're looking for. That's the trouble with these new grants. You don't know what their angle is, and nine times out of ten, neither do they! There's a Cerlith idiom. 'Derrah connoch tree.' It doesn't really translate, but I suppose it means 'Persistence will be rewarded'. (*Beat.*) Load of old bollocks really, isn't it?

NANGARRA: Is it?

GAIL: Well I've been arguing the case for Cerlith for nearly twenty years and I'm still waiting for mine. Reward that is.

NANGARRA: I didn't know you were a Cerlith speaker.

GAIL: Why? Don't I look the type?

NANGARRA: Your accent...

GAIL: What about it?

NANGARRA: Well, you haven't really got one.

GAIL: Years of living in London. The city robs you of it.

NANGARRA: You were born...?

GAIL: In the middle of absolute bloody nowhere. I was raised Cerlith. It was the only language I really spoke until I went to secondary school.

NANGARRA: That must've been a culture shock?

GAIL: It was only when I went away that I realised how bad my English was. Immigrant English. I'm sure people thought I was backward. It took me a long time to become fully, properly bilingual. Even when I'd left university I used to lapse into Cerlith. My husband used to laugh when I couldn't remember the English word for a straightforward object around the flat, you know? I'd be gabbling away and suddenly, wouldn't know the word for 'kettle', or 'rolling pin'. For no apparent reason, I wouldn't be able to find the word... it'd just drop out of my head. I could tell him in Cerlith of course, but that wouldn't have meant a bloody thing.

NANGARRA: He doesn't speak your language?

GAIL: John's from Surrey. We met at University. He knows a few words... picked them up when we went back to the island for holidays... but, well, he was always too busy to learn. He's a surgeon... works long hours.

NANGARRA: So your children don't...

GAIL: No. When they were babies I used to talk to them in Cerlith all the time, when it was just me at home, and they started to pick it up, they were doing well.... Duncan, my oldest boy, talks of learning one day, but David's not interested. He's living in Tokyo now. Teaching English as a foreign language. (*Beat.*) Do you have children?

NANGARRA: Not yet.

GAIL: Married?

NANGARRA: Divorced. My husband wanted to stay in the city. I wanted to go home. Help keep the language strong, y'know?

GAIL: I talked of going back, but there would've been no job for John... not on his salary anyway... and well... after a while you get comfortable, don't you? When the kids were out of my hair I took a post at the Linguistics Department, and suddenly my plan to return seemed so... unachievable.

NANGARRA: You'll never know, will you?

GAIL: Pardon?

NANGARRA: If you'd tried to go back things might have worked out differently.

GAIL: But life swept me along a different path.

NANGARRA: Yeah, and I suppose it helps if you really want to do it too.

GAIL glares at NANGARRA. AMOS enters.

AMOS: Thank God that's over. I could feel myself sweating. I was standing there, hoping, praying, they couldn't see me sweating... and the more I thought about it, the more I sweated.

NANGARRA: How d'you go?

AMOS: I survived.

GAIL: Are the seven dwarves in good spirits?

AMOS: Who? What? Oh. They seemed nice enough. Except the Estonian woman on the far left. Didn't smile the entire time and asked the most complicated question. (*Beat. Of his sweating:*) Can you see patches?

GAIL: Typical. You give them democracy, soap opera, and more blue denim than they can shake a stick at and they're still not happy. Wish me luck. (*She exits.*)

AMOS: Alright?

NANGARRA: Been better.

AMOS: Have you heard from home?

NANGARRA: Still no change.

Blackout.

Scene Eight

GAIL gives her presentation to the panel.

GAIL: The biggest threat to Cerlith is the outward migration of its speakers from the language's heartland. The last census showed there were just over fifty thousand Cerlith speakers living in the sample area as a whole, a drop of almost fifteen thousand. Naturally, some of that figure will be due to natural mortality, but a frightening percentage of it is due to the movement of Cerlith speakers away from the language's heartland to look for work.

The project I have been advising the Cerlith Language Trust with is an economic project to create job opportunities in areas that have traditionally been strong centres for Cerlith. An Asian technologies company has expressed a desire to locate its new European production base in a rural area where forty per cent of the population speaks Cerlith. The financial award you are offering would enable the Cerlith Language Trust to secure Asdaq's relocation and thus stem the flow of further outward migration. In doing so, we can hopefully reverse language decline before its too late.

The European Union has committed eight hundred thousand Euros to the scheme if the remaining sixty-seven-point-eight per cent of funds can be raised. With your grant, this target would be met and... (*Beat.*) Pardon?

(*Beat.*) Sixty-seven-point-four per cent? (*Beat.*) No, the figure is sixty-seven-point-eight. (*Back on track.*) The European contribution and... (*Beat.*) Yes. I'll be certain to double check.

Right. Where was I?

Blackout.

Scene Nine

JOEL prepares to give his presentation to the panel.

JOEL: The experiment will initially take place in two Native American languages. Mandaya and Yarru. Each community will be able to programme their set-top satellite box with their favoured language. Mandaya speakers select Mandaya, and Yarru, Yarru. The programme they choose to view is then immediately delivered to them in that language. The project is unique because as well as providing a much-needed indigenous broadcasting experience to speakers of these languages it will also create job opportunities for native speakers. Naturally, they will be needed to make programmes and in many cases will be required to translate scripts from English into their mother tongues. This project has real promise. And if successful, ladies and gentlemen, could embrace other languages America-wide.

Blackout.

Scene Ten

AMOS sits in the hotel suite alone. JOEL enters. AMOS jumps to his feet and sucks his stomach in.

AMOS: All done? Pretty painless, isn't it, really?

JOEL comes forward and starts shuffling his papers away into a briefcase.

AMOS: How d'you think it went? Well, impossible to tell, isn't it? Unless you're a mind-reader. Which I'm not. Although my mother says my grandmother had the gift, and they say it runs in families don't they? (*He grinds to an embarrassed halt.*)

JOEL: I'm quietly confident.

AMOS: That's all you can be, isn't it? Confident. This is the first time I've presented a project for such a large grant. If I don't get the funding, I'll put it down to experience, and try again next time. Maybe one day I'll be as successful as you.

JOEL: Excuse me?

AMOS: You must have a knack. You've secured funding from panels on a number of occasions. And I'm sure even you weren't successful on your first attempt.

JOEL smiles at AMOS.

AMOS: Or maybe you were. Were you?

JOEL: You talk a lot, don't you?

AMOS: Sorry. Am I rambling? I'm rambling, aren't I? I do that. I don't mean to, but I do. Can't stop myself. Tongue starts flapping and I'm away.... You should tell me to shut up. Really. All my friends do. It's the only way to stop me. Nangarra tells me to shut up all the time. When I get carried away, she's the first to tell me to put a cork, in it.

JOEL: I'm sure she is.

AMOS: Sorry?

JOEL: I can't imagine Nangarra ever minces her words.

AMOS: She can't afford to. If you want to get anything done you've got to shout the loudest and push the hardest.

JOEL: An agitator.

AMOS: She's committed to promoting Gurru Gurru. Even now when her mother's sick, she's here, trying to win the grant.

JOEL: What's wrong with her?

AMOS: Who? Oh, Nan's Mum. Cancer. Nangarra talks about getting her treated in America. There's a clinic or something, but she can't travel, can't afford to travel, and from what I understand, it's a matter of weeks before she passes away. But Nangarra's still here. Still fighting.

JOEL: I had no idea.

AMOS: And when she does go, die I mean, it's going to hit Nan hard. She'll be the only one then... the only one in her family that is, that speaks Gurru Gurru.

JOEL: Is there nobody else?

AMOS: None that speak the language. Her father died when she was a baby – alcohol. Her sisters were taken into care before she was born. Raised as white girls in white families. Her brother died five years ago. Walked into the wrong pub in Brisbane and didn't walk out again. 'Course, there are cousins and close family friends, but nobody who speaks Gurru Gurru. She'll have to go up country to speak her language.

JOEL: Where exactly?

AMOS: There are pockets of speakers throughout central Queensland. Bush people.

JOEL: Who says?

AMOS: Nangarra. She's the authority on the language.

JOEL: So I hear.

GAIL enters.

GAIL: They're not still talking, are they? You'd think they'd bore themselves silly after two hours.

JOEL: Leave our Valium, at home, did we?

GAIL: Fuck off. You know I can't stand the hanging around. Listen to the presentation, read the supporting literature, and get on with making a decision. Where's Nangarra?

AMOS: Still in there, I'm afraid.

GAIL: Oh, marvellous. So that means we won't get an answer until...

JOEL: They'll have lunch first.

AMOS: And then they'll take at least an hour, I'd've thought, to discuss...

JOEL: At least.

GAIL: Bastards. Well I'm not hanging around any longer than I have to. Joel? Fancy slipping out for a quick nibble?

JOEL: Now?

GAIL: Why not? I could do with a drink.

AMOS: Would you mind if I joined you? I haven't eaten all day. Nerves, I guess.

Pause. GAIL struggles with this new idea.

GAIL: No. 'Course not. The more the merrier.

They head towards the door, and the telephone rings.

JOEL: I'll get it.

AMOS and GAIL exit. JOEL answers the phone.

JOEL: Yes? (*Beat.*) No, she's not here at the moment. Can I take a message. (*Beat.*) Jen. Anything else? (*Beat.*) No, I'll tell her. (*He hangs up and exits.*)

Blackout.

Scene Eleven

NANGARRA gives her presentation to the panel.

NANGARRA: The massacre, and forced relocation of my people to reservations, was the first blow to an estimated two hundred and fifty aboriginal languages and eight hundred dialects, including my own language, Gurru Gurru. Allied with the rapid modernisation of our country and an increasing reliance on English for economic purposes, Australia's indigenous languages were quickly eroded. Government refused to acknowledge the languages for many years. Indeed they refused to acknowledge the indigenous peoples as human beings even, and officially referred to us as 'fauna' until 1967. How on earth, therefore, could we have our own languages?

It's from this bleak picture that I propose an ambitious plan to resurrect Gurru Gurru from the base of over two hundred and fifty speakers it has today, to more than one thousand in ten years and four thousand in twenty years. I argue that in today's modern world, to reward the learning of a language with financial reward, is not an artificial way of stimulating the growth of a language. In my community alone, the unemployment rate among Gurru Gurru men is fifty per cent. Why not, therefore pay these men to spend their days in the classroom learning Gurru Gurru? Learning their own language, which was after all, denied them. As my mother says, 'We gotta keep our language strong. It shows who we are, what we are. Language is part of us, deep inside. Without it... we're nothing.'

Blackout.

Scene Twelve

NANGARRA sits in the hotel suite alone. AMOS enters.

AMOS: Have you seen them?

NANGARRA: Punch and Judy?

AMOS: Joel and Gail.

NANGARRA: Why? Has the panel reached a decision?

AMOS: No. I lost them. We were heading out for something to eat. I went to the toilet, left them in the lobby, but by the time I got back, they'd gone. I checked the hotel restaurant, even popped into a couple of bars down the road, but... nothing.

NANGARRA: Two's company, eh?

AMOS: You're wrong about those two.

NANGARRA: Am I?

AMOS: Yeah, Joel would never go with someone so...

NANGARRA: Careful.

AMOS: Mature. I can't see it.

NANGARRA: Oh, Amos.

AMOS: Okay, okay. Maybe I just don't want to think about it. The squelching. (*Beat.*) How d'you get on?

NANGARRA: It was all going fine until I started talking about murder and genocide. I should've known these respectable panelists wouldn't have the stomach for a drop of blood.

AMOS: At least it's over. When're you headed home?

NANGARRA: Soon as they release us. I'm starting to wonder now whether I should've bothered.

AMOS: You got short-listed, you could win.

NANGARRA: Don't you feel depressed? When you think how much this has cost to set up – airfares, accommodation in a five-star hotel... they could've spent this budget on propping up a small endangered language for five years alone!

AMOS: This is how the system works.

NANGARRA: The system sucks. Power to the ones who buck the system. Remember that Warell woman? I'm starting to think she had the right idea. Pick your children up and walk off into the desert. Just walk away. Bring them up pure. Maybe that is the only true way to save language.

AMOS: Extreme.

NANGARRA: Effective.

AMOS: God, you are depressed.

NANGARRA: Tired, Amos. Just tired of it all.

AMOS hugs NANGARRA. GAIL and JOEL enter talking animatedly.

AMOS: Where did you two get to?

GAIL: Sorry, Amos. We must've lost you.

JOEL: Have you heard?

AMOS: I waited for half an hour.

NANGARRA: Heard what?

GAIL: I'm sorry. We couldn't find you.

JOEL: The panel's made a decision.

GAIL: We've got to go down to the meeting room to hear who's been awarded the grant.

AMOS: Oh God.

NANGARRA: Now?

JOEL: Moment of truth.

GAIL: Soon as, yes.

JOEL: By the way Nangarra, someone called for you.

AMOS: Here goes everything. (*He exits.*)

NANGARRA: When?

JOEL: Couple of hours ago.

GAIL: See you down there. (*She exits.*)

JOEL: Jen. Said you were to call home as soon as possible.

NANGARRA races for the phone.

JOEL: You were in the interview, otherwise I'd have come to fetch you...

NANGARRA is waiting for an answer on the phone. JOEL exits.

NANGARRA: Jen? What... (*Beat.*) When? (*Beat.*) No, sorry, thinking. Yeah, I'll be back as soon as I get a plane. (*Beat.*) No, don't arrange anything. Just tell everyone, yeah? Get the family together. (*She stands in shock. She hangs up.*)

Blackout.

Act Two

Scene One

NANGARRA sits in silence in the hotel suite coming to terms with the news she's just received. GAIL enters; clearly riled.

GAIL: I don't know why we bother. All the preparation, effort, energy... and to them it's just a game. Well, that's it. Next time they can get someone else to make a twat of themselves. I don't need this. I'm the head of a department. I don't need to get fucked around like this.

NANGARRA: You didn't win?

GAIL: Of course I didn't win. The smug bastards make me sick. Sitting up there on the stage playing fucking power games.

NANGARRA: Who *did* they give the grant to?

GAIL: That's my point. They didn't. After all the preparation, all the work... they failed to reach a majority decision. It's a farce. When news spreads about this we'll be a laughing stock.

NANGARRA: No decision?

GAIL: Seven allegedly intelligent men and women and they couldn't come up with a pissing answer.

NANGARRA: What happens now?

GAIL: Christ knows. I walked out. I couldn't listen to any more of their... shit.

AMOS enters.

AMOS: Did Gail tell you? They couldn't make a decision.

GAIL: Did the bastards come up with anymore excuses after I left?

AMOS: They expanded on their reasons.

GAIL: More waffle.

AMOS: Unable to make a decision as a group they decided to let another consortium make the choice.

GAIL: So we've got to go through it again?

AMOS: Not exactly.

GAIL: Then what?

AMOS: Give me five minutes and I'll explain Gail. (*Beat.*) The panel's decided, since they can't make a decision, that the power over which project should be awarded the funds, ought to be left in our hands.

NANGARRA: They want us to...

GAIL: Fight it out amongst ourselves! Bastards!

AMOS: They thought it was the only way forward. It seems

the battle was over three of the languages. One dropped out pretty early on, but the vote was split over three.

GAIL: Which ones?

AMOS: I don't know. Joel was trying to find out when I left. Turns out he knows the board's secretary.

NANGARRA: Why doesn't that surprise me?

JOEL enters.

GAIL: Did you find out what the bastards are fucking playing at?

JOEL: I'd forgotten how much you swear when you're angry, Gail.

GAIL: Fuck off, Joel. Just tell us what the bastards said.

JOEL: I'm sorry, Gail. You're out of the running. Fell at the first hurdle. Nangarra got one vote. Amos three, and I... well, you can do the math. After four rounds of voting, the figures weren't shifting, they were deadlocked. This started some pretty fierce arguing. My friend says most of the debate surrounded the Estonian delegate who was supporting Nangarra. Both sides were trying to get her to shift her allegiance and break the tie.

AMOS: But she wouldn't?

JOEL: Dynamite wouldn't have moved her. Things got worse when the Brazilian delegate angrily accused the stubborn Estonian of being, 'bitterly dogmatic.' By the time the phrase had gone from the Portugese translator into French, via the Polish translator and then into Estonian, our stubborn friend was being called, 'a difficult bitch.' Amidst the frantic conversations in the translators' gallery the term '*dog*matic' was somewhat misunderstood.

GAIL: Shits!

JOEL: There was no persuading the Estonian woman from there on. The chair became so frustrated by the discussion that when somebody said, 'We might as well let them decide for themselves', she put the idea to the panel. They voted, and four to three came down in favour of the idea.

GAIL: So, we have to choose which one of us gets the money?

JOEL: By tomorrow evening. Otherwise applications are re-opened, a new panel convened and we'll have to go through it again.

AMOS: How can we choose between four languages?

GAIL: That's the panel's problem, isn't it? You can't! Choose one winner and by default the other three are condemned. What they're really asking us to decide is which of our four languages lives, and which ones die!

JOEL: Three languages. Cerlith, since it didn't have any support in the discussion room, drops out. But Gail still gets to vote. We all have to vote, but naturally can't support our own languages. That way, someone definitely wins.

AMOS: If we want to play along.

JOEL: If we don't, the money won't be allocated and we all lose.

Pause.

GAIL: Bastard shits.

Blackout.

Scene Two

GAIL's hotel room. An angry GAIL enters, followed moments later by JOEL.

JOEL: Whoever said this was going to be a regular conference got it wrong I guess.

GAIL: You sound glad.

JOEL: I'm surprised. And a little amused.

GAIL: We should complain.

JOEL: There's no time.

GAIL: They've changed the rules. We should object.

JOEL: It's the inaugural year. There's no precedent.

GAIL: What they're doing is unfair.

JOEL: Someone might as well take the money.

GAIL: Unjust.

JOEL: I don't know why you're so worked up Gail. Maybe it's because you didn't do your math. (*Beat.*) Look, whatever their selection method, it's obvious you didn't stand a chance of winning. Not one person on the panel supported your idea. Please? Give it up.

GAIL glares at JOEL.

GAIL: Another victory for Joel Stuart.

JOEL: We hope so.

GAIL: Hope is the only thing in your way?

JOEL: Hope, Amos and Nangarra.

GAIL: What makes you think you've got my support?

JOEL: Who else would you vote for?

Beat.

GAIL: I'm finished, Joel. This is my last conference.

JOEL: I know it's disappointing but...

GAIL: The Cerlith Language Trust gave me a warning. If I didn't get support for my proposals at this conference they'd be looking for a new advisor.

JOEL: They were just talking tough. Nobody's got your experience and...

GAIL: Experience of failure isn't a quality people go looking for.

JOEL: You know more about Cerlith than any other linguist in the world.

GAIL: Knowledge doesn't mean a thing when you can't attract funding. Money's all that matters these days, Joel. And I can't raise it anymore. I'm past it.

JOEL: You're far from finished. You'll still teach.

GAIL: Oh, yes! I'll catch the train into the city every morning, teach the same sullen students every day, and go home to the same husband every night, have the same conversation before going to sleep in different beds. (*Beat.*) But I've always wanted more. Inside I'm still as ambitious as I was twenty years ago. I can't believe my career's reached a dead end.

JOEL: It hasn't. There'll be positions for you on panels, guest lectures...

GAIL: As if.

JOEL: Sure! In fact, we're looking for someone at Burton to run a lecture series in the Fall. The position is still vacant. Why don't you take it?

GAIL: You don't have to be kind, Joel.

JOEL: I'm not. It's two weeks of lectures. Any subject you want. You're knowledge is important Gail.

JOEL kisses GAIL.

JOEL: Look, I know we get together at these events... orgasm, leave and don't see one another for months, years... but you are important to me. I mean it. Valuable.

Beat.

GAIL: California, eh?

JOEL: The offer's on the table. What do you say?

Beat. GAIL smiles.

GAIL: Well, our winters can be bitterly cold.

Blackout.

Scene Three

A golf green. AMOS and JOEL have come out for a game of golf. They have a golf bag on a trolley. JOEL looks the part, but AMOS doesn't. JOEL enters and sets up his next shot. AMOS joins him on the green.

JOEL: You didn't have to join me, y'know? I just thought it might be a nice thing for us guys to do.

AMOS: It is. I mean, I've been thinking about taking it up

for a while, but...

JOEL: Too busy, huh?

AMOS: Not enough hours in the day.

JOEL: You should make time. It's very relaxing.

JOEL takes his shot. They watch it fly, then land.

AMOS: Hey! You're good. Really good.

JOEL: I know. Been playing since I was a kid. It gets easier.

AMOS: Am I supposed to believe you?

JOEL: The last hole you played was better than your first, wasn't it? How many shots did you take on that?

AMOS: Erm, thirteen.

JOEL: Thought you were going for the world record. Want to set up your ball?

AMOS fiddles in the golf bag for a ball and a tee. He sets up.

JOEL: Been an unusual conference, hasn't it?

AMOS: Weird. That was the last thing I was expecting them to say today. I mean, it's such an unorthodox move. I was stunned by what was coming out of their mouths. 'Unusual' isn't the word you'd use to describe something like that. I'm not sure what the word is, but it's more than 'unusual'. It's greater. It's a...

JOEL: Amos?

AMOS: Hmm?

JOEL: Shut up. (*Beat.*) You did give me permission.

AMOS smiles.

JOEL: They've passed the responsibility on to us. Some would say it was a cop out, others might say it was a smart move. After all, we're four intelligent people with a strong knowledge of endangered languages and the problems they face. Why shouldn't we make the choice? I think the panel's empowered us, Amos. I think they've actually done us a favour.

AMOS is holding a putter.

JOEL: You probably don't want to use that to strike the ball. It's the putter, remember?

AMOS: Oh, yeah.

JOEL: Try the five iron.

AMOS looks confused.

JOEL: It's the one with the number five written on it.

AMOS exchanges the putter for a five iron.

JOEL: I haven't had a chance yet to read your proposal thoroughly. The papers arrived in my room an hour before we were coming out here, but I thought your proposal, what I read of it, was fascinating. I really did. Congratulations.

AMOS: Thank you.

JOEL: When young speakers reject a language, the language is fucked, yeah?

AMOS: Right.

JOEL: Fucked hard, if you know what I mean?

AMOS: Yeah. I do.

JOEL: So the idea of creating a pop band which will sing in Thiai is a very sensible and strong idea which I'm sure will help sheer up the Thiai language. Young speakers will start to embrace their language and actually *speak* it. Really, Amos, I think yours is probably the best idea on the table.

AMOS: Really?

JOEL: Really. Which is why I've decided to support your idea. (*Beat.*) You've got my vote.

AMOS is stunned.

AMOS: Me? You're supporting me?

JOEL: Sure.

AMOS: Well, I'm flattered. Truly. I mean, for an eminent linguist such as yourself to...

JOEL: All I expect is that you show me the same courtesy.

Pause.

JOEL: That won't be a problem, will it?

AMOS: Well, I... haven't read the papers yet, I don't know what everyone else is proposing.

JOEL: I know you and Nangarra are friends.

AMOS: It's not just that, it's...

JOEL: I know you've got a history, and I'm sure she's going to support you in the final vote.

AMOS: Well...

JOEL: Isn't she?

AMOS: Probably.

JOEL: All I ask is that you vote for me. I don't want to be the only one with no votes, y'know? I'd lose so much face if I returned home a loser. I'd get laughed out of the department. Do you want to take your shot now?

AMOS: Yes. 'Course.

AMOS prepares for his shot. He squats down and steadies himself.

JOEL watches.

JOEL: You need to relax your shoulders. Open your stance a little. Your legs need to be wider. Here, like this.

JOEL goes behind him and takes control. He physically puts AMOS into a better position. JOEL stands behind AMOS showing him how to use the club.

JOEL: Okay? Now grip the club hard. There you go.

JOEL is standing behind AMOS pressed up close to him with his hands gripped over AMOS's hands. JOEL's head is practically on AMOS's shoulder.

JOEL: Swing the club back.

AMOS is in heaven.

JOEL: And when you're ready, hit the ball.

JOEL steps back. Concentrating hard, AMOS hits the ball. They watch it fly, and land.

JOEL: What was that like?

AMOS: Fantastic. I mean, thank you.

JOEL: I like you, Amos. I like your project. Nangarra's going to be supporting you too. She won't mind if you don't vote for her. Particularly if not doing so means you get unanimous support.

AMOS: Why? Is Gail voting for me?

JOEL: Gail likes you Amos. She thinks that you, unlike your golf ball, will go far.

Beat.

JOEL: So? What do you say?

AMOS: Sorry?

JOEL: Will you vote for me?

AMOS: Well...

JOEL: Put it this way. I have a vacancy at Burton in the Fall. A lecture series. Very prestigious. Particularly for a young academic like yourself. If everything goes to plan tomorrow I wouldn't hesitate in offering you the position, Amos. (*Beat.*) Shall we move on?

JOEL walks away. AMOS flustered by these last moments, follows.

Blackout.

Scene Four

NANGARRA is sitting on the sofa reading a thick spiral bound report. GAIL enters. NANGARRA looks up from the report.

GAIL: Not exactly bedtime reading, is it? But then again, if the whole point of bedtime reading is to send you to sleep...

NANGARRA: You're finished?

GAIL: I'm a fast reader. Comes with years of reading the scribblings of my students.

NANGARRA: I'm mid-way through Joel's proposal.

GAIL: Amazing, isn't it? How Joel's got so much front?

NANGARRA: He's coming across like the Messiah. Sent here to save the dying languages of the Americas.

GAIL: Joel's nothing if not ambitious.

NANGARRA: He proposes a television channel for two languages, but rather than discussing the detail of how that channel will operate, be paid for, he goes on to paint his vision of the future where this single channel will broadcast in every native American language across the continent. That's not front. It's delusion.

GAIL: Every project Joel's ever come up with has been just as bold and innovative. He creates grand plans. He endeavours to make them happen. Most of us are too inhibited to develop ideas on the same scale.

NANGARRA: Most of us know such plans would be unrealistic.

GAIL: Maybe Joel's got a different understanding of what reality is. You've got to admire him really.

Beat.

NANGARRA: I don't need to ask you who you intend to vote for tomorrow, do I?

GAIL: I think Joel's idea is very strong. I think all our ideas are very strong.

NANGARRA: But you're voting for Joel?

GAIL: What makes you say that?

NANGARRA: Well, for starters you're f... friends.

GAIL: So are you and Amos. Regardless of friendship Nangarra, I'll be choosing the project I think is most deserving. Won't you?

NANGARRA: Of course.

Pause.

GAIL: How's your mother?

NANGARRA: Why d'you ask?

GAIL: I heard she was ill.

NANGARRA: She's feeling better, thanks.

GAIL: Really? Joel told me she had terminal cancer. He was under the impression she was dying.

NANGARRA: Joel's mistaken. I spoke to her earlier.

GAIL: In Gurru Gurru?

NANGARRA: What else?

GAIL: That's right. Your mother and you are the only speakers left. In your family, that is.

NANGARRA: Who told you that?

GAIL: Joel.

NANGARRA: Joel seems to know a lot about me.

GAIL: He's very interested in you.

NANGARRA: Clearly.

GAIL: He thinks you're a very intelligent woman. (*Beat.*) I suppose he must be mistaken. About your mother, I mean. He must've misunderstood.

NANGARRA: Yes.

GAIL: I lost my mother five years ago. She had a massive stroke, and well... gone. (*Beat.*) It's funny, since I only saw her once or twice a year – because of the distance more than anything – I didn't think I'd be as devastated as I was. Oh, does that sound terrible? It isn't meant to. Really. I just didn't think I'd miss her as much as I did. Do. And since she's been gone, I hardly speak Cerlith anymore. We used to speak on the phone three times a week, and when she'd come to stay we'd speak it all day long. But now that she's dead, I hardly use it. And after forty something years, that's strange.

NANGARRA: Is there no one else you can talk with?

GAIL: Colleagues, occasionally. Distant relations, once in a blue moon. (*Beat.*) I know you look at me and see a woman who isn't committed to her language, Nangarra. But just because I don't live in the community and my children don't speak Cerlith, doesn't mean I don't feel the loss. My heart sinks every time I hear of a drop in the number of speakers the same as yours must when you hear of another Gurru Gurru speaker passing away. It affects me. Here.

NANGARRA splutters. She can't hold back her tears anymore. She covers her eyes with her hands.

GAIL: Are you...?

NANGARRA: Fine. Really.

GAIL: Are you sure?

NANGARRA: I'm just tired. Feel like I haven't slept in weeks. And the pressure of the last few days hasn't helped.

GAIL: I have some tablets you could take.

NANGARRA dries her eyes.

GAIL: They're herbal. Not addictive.

NANGARRA laughs at GAIL's footnote.

NANGARRA: I just need to go home. I need to go home and rest.

AMOS enters.

GAIL: Back so soon?

NANGARRA: Where've you been?

AMOS: Playing golf. With Joel.

GAIL: D'you know where he is, Amos? I was hoping to have a quick word.

AMOS: He went to his room. He had some calls to...

GAIL: Well, I might go and see him then. Catch up. I'll see you both later.

GAIL exits.

NANGARRA: Golf with Joel Stuart? Sounds like a date to me. Did he score a hole in one?

AMOS: Evil imagination!

NANGARRA: He'll be buying you flowers next. Mark my words Amos, there's more to Joel than meets the eye. Why else has he asked me to meet him for drinks tonight?

Blackout.

Scene Five

JOEL's bedroom. JOEL is busy working on his lap top. There's a knock at the door. Then another. A preoccupied JOEL eventually gets up and answers it. He opens the door to reveal a playful GAIL standing there with a bottle of champagne and two glasses.

GAIL: So this is where you're hiding?

GAIL enters.

GAIL: Thought I'd come and help you celebrate. (*She sits on the edge of the bed and starts to open the bottle of champagne.*)

JOEL: Celebrate what?

GAIL: Well, I take it everything went to plan with Amos.

JOEL: Yes, I think so...

GAIL: Then you've got the votes you need to win the prize. Congratulations. (*Of the bottle:*) No matter how many of these buggers I open, it never gets any easier...

JOEL: Listen, Gail. I don't want to be a...

GAIL: If you're hungry we could order room service.

JOEL: No, thanks. I've eaten.

GAIL: Me too, but I'm still starving. Maybe we could split something?

JOEL: No, Gail...

GAIL: A piece of pie perhaps?

JOEL: I've got e-mails to answer.

GAIL: We can get two forks.

JOEL: Proofs to check.

GAIL: Or cake! What about a slice of cake?

JOEL: I don't want any fucking cake, okay?

Pause.

JOEL: Sorry.

GAIL: You've an aversion to chocolate. That's alright.

JOEL: I shouldn't have shouted.

GAIL: You didn't want cake, Joel. It's not a big deal. I shouldn't have forced the issue.

JOEL: You didn't. I snapped and I apologise....

GAIL: Some people like sweet things. Clearly you're not one of them.

Pause. GAIL gets up to leave.

GAIL: I shouldn't have come.

JOEL: Gail...

GAIL: I shouldn't have disturbed you.

JOEL: It's okay. Gail...

JOEL stops GAIL from going.

JOEL: I'm sorry I shouted. It's been a tough day. You know how highly I think of you. You're the last person I want to offend. Stay?

Beat.

GAIL: I've been thinking about your offer. California. (*Beat.*) Well, I think I should come for an entire semester. It's what I need. A change of scene.

JOEL: What about John?

GAIL: John can look after himself. I'll take a sabbatical. And if things work out, maybe I can stay on. There are always new positions aren't there? Your staff is growing?

JOEL: Yes, but...

GAIL: We could see how it goes, couldn't we? If you win this grant, if you get the votes you need that is, the department's going to expand. You'll need people you can rely on. Like me. I think it could work? Don't you?

JOEL (*giving in*): Yes, Gail.

JOEL kisses GAIL.

GAIL: What have you got planned for tonight?

JOEL: Not a lot. I need to e-mail some people, make some calls....

GAIL: Do you want to call by later? To continue the celebration?

JOEL: Sure.

GAIL: I'm glad we're friends Joel. I like that you confide in me. We make a good team. (*She moves to the door.*) Maybe later we can discuss my sabbatical. Work out some details? Suddenly, the future doesn't seem so grim. (*She leaves.*)

Blackout.

Scene Six

The hotel suite. AMOS is clearing away papers when GAIL enters to collect her jacket. There's a spring in her step.

GAIL: Still ploughing your way through the mountain of paper Amos?

AMOS: Yes, there's so much to consider when making a decision like this isn't there?

GAIL smiles knowingly.

GAIL: Did you enjoy your game of golf with Joel?

AMOS: I reckon I was getting the hang of it by the eighteenth hole.

Beat.

AMOS: Look Gail, I've been meaning to tell you how sorry I am that the panel ruled you out of this process. I know how I'd feel if I was in your shoes and I just wanted to say...

GAIL: Fuck it!

AMOS: Oh. I thought you'd be disappointed.

GAIL: Not at all. It's a relief really. I've decided to resign my position with the Cerlith Language Trust. It's time to move on.

AMOS: And you're happy about that?

GAIL: Delighted. Joel's offered me the chance to lecture at Burton, you see. Initially it's just a two week lecture series, but he's hoping to keep me on for a semester or two. It sounds like a very progressive department. I'm very excited about it. Thrilled, in fact.

AMOS: Me too.

GAIL: Pardon?

AMOS: Oh, don't you know? Joel's invited me to lecture at Burton too. Next Fall.

GAIL: He has?

AMOS: He said he had a vacancy he couldn't fill to his satisfaction. I didn't realise there was enough work for the two of us. But that's great. It'll be nice to have a familiar...

GAIL realises she's been betrayed. She goes to leave. Her head's spinning.

AMOS: Joel won't be in his room.

GAIL stops in her tracks.

AMOS: Nangarra said they had some pressing business to discuss. At least, that's what she told me.

GAIL glares at AMOS and leaves.

Blackout.

Scene Seven

The roof terrace of a wine bar in central Cardiff. JOEL sits at a table, waiting. NANGARRA arrives. JOEL notices her immediately.

JOEL: I was starting to think you'd stood me up.

NANGARRA: Sorry, I was reading your report. (*She sits.*)

JOEL: Good read, huh?

NANGARRA: If you like fiction.

JOEL: Whoa! Don't pull any punches do you?

NANGARRA: Well, I assume that's what you wanted to talk to me about, isn't it? Your proposal. My vote.

JOEL: And something tells me you've already made up your mind.

NANGARRA: Can't vote for myself. Gail's out of the race. You've written the biggest load of bullshit I've read in a long time. There isn't a lot of choice, is there?

JOEL: What is it you find so objectionable about my idea, Nangarra?

NANGARRA: Where do I start?

JOEL: Wherever you want to.

NANGARRA: Okay. The share holdings.

JOEL: What about them?

NANGARRA: The sums don't add up. You say that the companies providing the technology will have shares in the television station, and that the communities you broadcast to will also have shares, as will the company selling the set top boxes...

JOEL: And your point is?

NANGARRA: When all's said and done, this still leaves a twenty-percent company share unaccounted for.

JOEL: That's correct. It'll be held in trust for future communities that join the project.

NANGARRA: Held in trust by whom?

JOEL: A trustee who will use his discretion to award the remaining shares when the time is right.

NANGARRA: And who is this trustee?

JOEL: I am.

NANGARRA: And if you choose not to award any further shares, you will control those shares yourself, correct?

JOEL: There's nothing illegal about this set up, Nangarra.

NANGARRA: But plenty that's immoral.

JOEL: I don't understand your problem. I'm working to set up a television station for lesser-used languages in the US. Forgive me, I thought I was doing a good thing.

NANGARRA: On paper. But what happens when those languages die, Joel?

JOEL: The station is set up entirely for that purpose, Nangarra. To ensure they don't die.

NANGARRA: But nothing's certain. If those languages die, or the languages lose so many speakers that broadcasting in those languages becomes insupportable, what happens to your TV station? The TV station you have shares in?

JOEL: This is entirely hypothetical.

NANGARRA: With the infrastructure in place you will have a TV company in your hands that you could sell to any buyer. What happens to your vision then? It broadcasts English language pop music twenty-four hours a day? It plays kids' cartoons non-stop morning, noon and night? (*Beat.*) I've looked beyond the pretty words and glossy graphics, Joel. I can see that at the end of this project there'll be a windfall for the man who set it up.

JOEL: You think you've figured me out, don't you?

NANGARRA: Pretty much.

JOEL: Well, let me give you this scenario. I launch my TV station, which for your information I intend to do whether it's with this money or somebody else's, and I intend to make it a success...

NANGARRA: With private money from multinational advertisers?

JOEL: If that's what it takes to broadcast in two fragile endangered languages, yes. What matters is establishing a network which will serve a number of speakers of languages which at present have no broadcasting services whatsoever.

NANGARRA: But what sort of service will you offer on the budgets you propose?

JOEL: The station will, I grant you, be run on a shoestring.

NANGARRA: You haven't got any money to make programmes, Joel!

JOEL: As I say in the report, 'We will buy programming from around the world.' Animation, documentaries, drama, all dubbed or subtitled into endangered languages.

NANGARRA: What kind of drama?

JOEL: Quality drama.

NANGARRA: Such as? Give me specifics not generalisations.

JOEL: Christ.

NANGARRA: Go on.

Beat.

JOEL: 'Cagney and Lacey.' 'Hart to Hart.' 'Knight Rider.'

NANGARRA laughs.

JOEL: I like 'Knight Rider'! What's wrong with 'Knight Rider'?

NANGARRA continues to laugh. JOEL relaxes.

NANGARRA: You think 'Knight Rider' will save Yarru?

JOEL: On the flight over here, Nangarra, I sat behind three teenage kids. When they wanted a drink they'd bleep the flight attendant, who'd come up the aisle, turn off the overhead light and ask them what it was they wanted. Together they'd say, 'Pepsi'. Not, 'I would like a glass of Pepsi, please.' No. There were no other words to hold up the request. Just, 'Pepsi.'

NANGARRA: What's your point?

JOEL: My point is we need language less and less, and therefore we need fewer languages. We're losing the war, Nangarra, but if broadcasting 'Knight Rider' in Yarru can keep the language alive for another eighty, or hundred years, then I'm willing to give it a shot.

NANGARRA: Sounds to me like you're in the wrong job.

JOEL: I didn't choose this line of work on a whim. Trust me, four years spent writing a PhD on tribal African dialects is not something you do on a whim.

NANGARRA: Then why did you?

JOEL: There's a nomadic tribe in the Sahara desert that has no word for cigarette, but twenty-six for heat. Twenty-six words to describe heat! That fact alone floors me. It stuns me when I think that there are concepts in this world that can never translate into English. Concepts I will never understand because my language doesn't have the words to describe them. That is why I do this. I do it because if we let languages that have been spoken for thousands of years slip away, we lose the history, culture and knowledge that are intrinsic to those languages. We lose so fucking much. Yet, because we can't define what we lose, point to it in material terms, and say, 'There you are! That's what's going out with the trash tomorrow unless you do something about it,' people don't understand. They don't understand what's being lost. (*Beat.*) Do you believe me?

NANGARRA: I want to, Joel. But when I read your report.... When I learn you're making deals with multi-million dollar companies, I become suspicious. When I hear you're buying episodes of 'Cagney and Lacey' in an effort to 'save' a language that's been spoken for tens of thousands of years... yes, I'm sceptical. I doubt you because you've represented twelve endangered languages in the last five years alone. You ask me to believe you when you tell me that you want to 'save' Mandaya and Yarru. But what am I to think when I learn in six months time you're working in Eastern Europe advising yet another government on how it should save its minority language?

JOEL: You should think I'm good at my job. (*Beat.*) Just because my approach to the problem is different, Nangarra, doesn't necessarily mean that it's wrong.

NANGARRA: A language doesn't exist unless it's spoken. You can broadcast 'Cagney and Lacey' in Mandaya twenty-four hours a day and there's no guarantee the language will survive. You've got to make sure the language is passed on to the next generation.

JOEL: Yes, and broadcasting in an endangered language gives it status...

NANGARRA: But there's no guarantee anyone will watch it! I can watch 'Cagney and Lacey' in English. Why do I want to watch it in Yarru too? In fact, why do I want to watch it at all?

(*Beat.*) Look, I don't think you're a bad man. You're not a terrible man.

JOEL: Thanks.

NANGARRA: I just think you could be a better man. (*Beat.*) I know how precious language is, Joel. If languages were rain forests the world would protect them. We'd protest. But when a language is under threat, most people do nothing. One language dies every two weeks, Joel. Isn't that the figure? Fifty-eight languages have only one living speaker. It's horrific.

JOEL: Fifty-seven. I thought the number was fifty-seven.

Beat.

NANGARRA: Statistics change. (*Beat.*) We've got to spend this money at the root of the problem. Not pouring it into the pockets of fat rich men so they can grow fatter. (*She drinks deeply.*)

JOEL: I know you're lying about the number of Gurru Gurru speakers, Nangarra. I know there aren't two hundred and fifty.

NANGARRA: Expert in Aboriginal Australia now are you?

JOEL: I spoke with Connie Matthews.

NANGARRA: I've never liked opportunists.

JOEL: Her arguments are quite convincing.

NANGARRA: If that's what you want to hear.

JOEL: Then how many speakers of Gurru Gurru are there? Show me their names. Show me the research. Twenty? Ten? Five? Three? One?

Beat.

NANGARRA: Gurru Gurru is a living language.

JOEL: I asked Connie whether she'd be interested in returning to Queensland with a team of my researchers to complete her analysis. I asked her to draw up a budget.

Unnoticed, GAIL enters. She sees NANGARRA and JOEL together. Beat. GAIL turns and leaves.

NANGARRA: What do you want from me?

JOEL: Your vote tomorrow.

NANGARRA: And then you'll leave me alone?

JOEL: I'm sure I can let Connie down gently.

NANGARRA considers the situation.

NANGARRA: When you called me here tonight I thought you were going to try and sleep with me.

JOEL: I considered it.

NANGARRA: But decided against it?

JOEL: I know better than to go swimming in choppy waters.

NANGARRA: You think I'm choppy?

JOEL: Calm isn't a word I'd necessarily use to describe you.

NANGARRA: '*Irri wallah, sirri wallah.*'

JOEL: What does that mean?

NANGARRA (*she smiles*): 'There's more to this big girl than her bounce.'

JOEL smiles.

Blackout.

Scene Eight

The next day. The lights come up on AMOS, JOEL, NANGARRA and GAIL in turn as they give their decisions.

AMOS: What? Do I write it down or do I... just tell you, yes? Alright. Well, after much consideration and thought... just say it, right? I have decided to support... Joel Stuart.

JOEL: My vote goes to... Nangarra Yinpungu.

NANGARRA: I'm supporting... Amos Fraser.

GAIL: No, I have decided, but first I would like to object to the way I've been treated by this panel. To eliminate me –

let me finish please – to eliminate me was unfair and unconstitutional, and I want this panel to know.... (*Beat.*) Alright, if that's how you feel about it. (*Beat.*) Amos Fraser. (*Beat.*) Yes, I'm sure.

Blackout.

Scene Nine

An hour later. The hotel suite. GAIL is packing away her briefcase. JOEL enters. GAIL looks up and sees him, before continuing with her packing.

GAIL: Did you know there was a University in Palma? Neither did I until today. 'Just met the lingusitics professor. He's offered me a lecture series. Be nice, won't it? Sea, sun, sangria... there's even talk I might get to do some work on the language of the Majorcans. There's always a bright side, isn't there?

JOEL: Gail? Why?

GAIL: Last night, while I was waiting for you in bed, I read your report. There were a few details I disagreed with, Joel. And I decided I couldn't, for professional reasons, do it.

JOEL: I don't understand. You promised.

GAIL: And you promised you'd come and see me.

JOEL: I was going to...

GAIL: But?

JOEL: I lay down to wait for an important call, and... y'know... fell asleep. I can't believe you switched votes. We were making plans. You were coming with me to the States. I thought we understood each other.

GAIL: You shouldn't have taken me for granted. You shouldn't have lied to me.

JOEL: What!

GAIL (*exploding*): Don't tell me you were sleeping when you were with Nangarra. What were you doing, eh? Offering her a lecture series at Burton too? Like you did with Amos, me, and God knows who else! You lie to me and expect me to give you my support? Maybe you really are deluded.

GAIL exits with her bag. As she passes through the door she is met by NANGARRA entering.

GAIL: You didn't vote for him either. Perhaps I underestimated you. (*She exits.*)

JOEL: Am I really such a terrible person?

NANGARRA: Amos is my friend. You said you could find the money elsewhere. I didn't think you were serious.

JOEL: Even after I said I'd get Connie Matthews to blow apart your research on Gurru Gurru?

NANGARRA: Connie Matthews doesn't frighten me, Joel.

Send her back. Waste your money. There are two hundred and fifty speakers of Gurru Gurru in Australia. Let her prove otherwise. I've nothing to hide.

AMOS enters.

JOEL: Amos, we need to talk.

AMOS: Sure.

JOEL (*goes to leave*): Goodbye Nangarra.

NANGARRA: Joel? Thank you.

JOEL exits.

NANGARRA: Another date?

AMOS: He wants to take me out for a beer to celebrate my winning the grant.

NANGARRA: So it *is* a date? I'm surprised. Wasn't he supposed to be voting for you too?

AMOS: He was. I mean, we agreed he would, but he came out for you instead. Maybe you're the one he wants to bed after all.

NANGARRA: Aren't you angry with him?

AMOS: He explained he knew I was going to walk it. He tried to page me last night but he couldn't find my number.

NANGARRA: Easy excuse.

AMOS: No, it's the truth. I don't own a pager. He's got some ideas for me. Pointers on how to improve the project.

NANGARRA: Sounds ominous.

AMOS: He's got a mate in LA who runs a recording studio. He's got this idea we could maybe record the band's tracks in English alongside Thiai... expand the market for the product.

NANGARRA: But isn't the idea of the band supposed to be that they sing in Thiai?

AMOS: Yes, and they will. But what harm can it do to make the music available in English too? It could be a money spinner. To support further projects, I mean.

NANGARRA: Amos...

AMOS: It's just an idea, Nan. I'm talking to him about it. I'm not selling out. I'm just looking at all the options. He's very well connected. He could help me. Y'know?

Pause.

NANGARRA: I should go.

AMOS: What time's your flight?

NANGARRA: Eight o'clock.

AMOS: It's been good to see you again.

They embrace.

AMOS: What's next in the pipeline?

NANGARRA: I don't know. Maybe I'll ease off the research and start thinking about that other project. The baby.

AMOS: Going to trap a man, are you?

NANGARRA: If that's the last option open to me. Bye, Amos.

NANGARRA leaves. AMOS walks around the room – very pleased with himself. Victorious, he whoops and punches the air. Success!

Blackout.

Scene Ten

NANGARRA stands alone talking to the audience. This could be a lecture, but we realise that it isn't when, mid-way, it is revealed that she's standing on red earth – barefoot.

NANGARRA: The woman took her children and left the reservation with nothing but the clothes they stood up in and a knife tucked into her waistband for cutting meat. They walked into the bush. They walked away from the outside world and cut themselves off from English, TV, and modern life. The next day, the woman's family were mad with worry. They started to look for her. Track her like a wallaby or goanna... but they couldn't find her. The woman had done well. The woman had covered her tracks. She had feared for her children. She had seen the other children on the reservation and worried. She saw them talking English, forgetting the old ways, wishing for a life in the city as a pop star, or racing car driver. The woman wanted her children to speak her language, to understand her culture's ways, to dream their own dreams. So taking her children by the hand she led them away, and raised them pure. (*She clutches her stomach. It's round, she's at least six months pregnant. She speaks to her child.*) *Iwi Marra. Ganga sirri gara. Iwi jarra ganga.* (*Beat.*) *Iwi jarra ganga.* (*She looks out at the audience.*) *Iwi Marra.*

Blackout.

The End.

Mother Tongue: The Story Behind the Play

The story of *Mother Tongue* is a long one. It started in 1998 when Wales Arts International invited me to visit Australia as part of the New Wales in New South Wales initiative. I spent nine months with the Australian National Playwrights' Centre and Sydney Theatre Company writing a play about Welsh identity and Australian soap opera called *Killing Kangaroos*. During this period I started to learn about Aboriginal Australian culture and was staggered to discover that the indigenous people of Australia once spoke over two hundred and fifty languages. The majority of these languages are now dead, and the Australian government is doing very little to protect the ones that continue to survive. I knew upon returning to Wales that this was something I was going to write about. In the months that followed I read extensively about the subject of endangered languages and the concept for *Mother Tongue* was born.

In 2000 I was awarded a playwright's bursary by the Arts Council of Wales to start work on the play (thank you, Anna Holmes) and a travel grant from the ever supportive Wales Arts International (thank you, Ceri Thomas). I returned to Australia in 2001 to meet speakers of the remaining Aboriginal languages and the linguists who are working to document and promote these languages. (Thanks particularly to those at the Batchelor Institute of Indigenous Tertiary Education in Alice Springs for allowing me to visit.) I also travelled to New Zealand where I met with Te Taura Whiri I Te Reo Maori (the Maori Language Commission) and a number of Maori playwrights, including Briar Grace Smith and the inspirational Hone Kouka. Before returning to Wales, I'd already started writing the play which was originally entitled *Lingua* and would become *Mother Tongue*.

A fragment of the play was read for the first time in New York by Helen Griffin and Darren Lawrence during the UK in NY arts festival (2001), and was completed in American playwright Kelly Stuart's apartment long after the festival was over. Kelly has been steadfast in her support of the play since I told her about the idea in 2000 and it is in large part to her that the play ever saw the light of day.

Another supporter has been Australian writer and director Rachel Hennessy, who directed a reading at the Pleasance, London, in 2002. Following this reading I received an invitation from the Lark Theatre in New York to present the play there in 2003 (thanks to Michael Johnson Chase and his cast) and was invited back the following year to present the play again (thanks to Linnet Taylor and her cast).

Also, in 2004, the play was read in Wellington as part of the New Zealand International Arts Festival. The invitation was extended by the festival's artistic director Carla Van Zon (whom I'd met on my travels in 2001) and the play was directed by Christian Penny at Te Whaea National Dance and Drama Centre (once again, thank you to the fantastic cast for bringing it to life).

And now finally, the play receives its first full production at Chapter, Cardiff. In a sense, it's come home. Following a series of rejections for funding to produce the play over the last three years, James Tyson has finally made it happen. James is one of the many who have supported the play over the years, and to everyone who's encouraged me to stick with it, I'd like to say thank you.

Particular thanks are due to Jeff Teare, Jane Dauncey, Tracy Spottiswoode, and everyone at Made In Wales, Chris Ricketts and Ceri Thomas at Wales Arts International, Lewis Davies at Parthian for reminding me that anything is possible, and to Paul Rees for putting up with it, and me.

Diolch yn fawr.

Roger Williams, Pen-bre, June 2005.

YIRRA
YAAKIN

YIRRA YAAKIN [Yir-r*aar*h Y*aar*h-kin] is Australia's leading Aboriginal theatre company, unequalled in innovation, excellence and cultural significance. Our priority is to ensure Aboriginal theatre remains under Aboriginal Control – providing opportunities for Aboriginal artists in all levels of creation and production. We operate within an International Indigenous arts context and seek to foster collaborations that have a strong cultural foundation to further support authentic Indigenous expressions.

www.yirrayaakin.asn.au